A Gift For:

Jacksen "J"man

From:

Wena ♡

*For Edward & Scarlett*
—G. S.

*For Timothy, with love*
—A. C.

Text copyright © 2009 by Gillian Shields
Illustrations copyright © 2009 by Anna Currey

This edition published in 2010 by Hallmark Books, a division of Hallmark Cards, Inc., under license from Bloomsbury U.S.A.
Visit us on the Web at Hallmark.com.

ISBN 978-1-59530-325-7
BOK1160

Printed and bound in China
JUL10

# When the World Is Ready for Bed

Gillian Shields

illustrated by Anna Currey

BLOOMSBURY

NEW YORK BERLIN LONDON

Hallmark

GIFT BOOKS

When the world
Is ready for bed,
The sky grows dark,
The sun glows red.

The little flowers
Shut their eyes,
The night birds sing
Their lullabies.

Supper's ready
In the pot—
Come and eat it
While it's hot.

Now clear the room
And tidy up;
There's a toy,
And here's a cup.

Let's talk about
The things you've done—
All the laughter,
All the fun.

Brush your teeth
And comb your hair.
Fold your clothes
Upon the chair.

Close the curtains,
Sleepyhead.
Find your blanket,
Cuddle Ted.

Pictures, stories,
One last look
At the tales
In one last book.

The lamp glows softly
On the stairs;
It's time for kisses,
Hugs, and prayers . . .

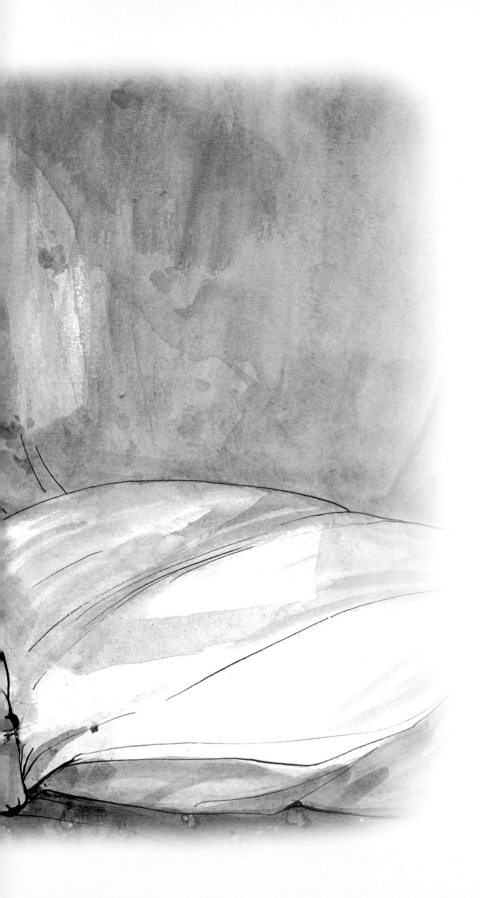

. . . And look! A star
Is shining bright,
To guard you
In the dreaming night.

Today has nearly
Slipped away;
Tomorrow brings
Another day.

Always lovely,
Always new,
Tomorrow's waiting
Just for you.

Did you enjoy this book?
Hallmark would love
to hear from you.

Please send your comments to:
Hallmark Book Feedback
P.O. Box 419034
Mail Drop 215
Kansas City, MO 64141

Or e-mail us at:
booknotes@hallmark.com